ANIMAL RESCUE
WILDLIFE PRESERVES

John Clendening

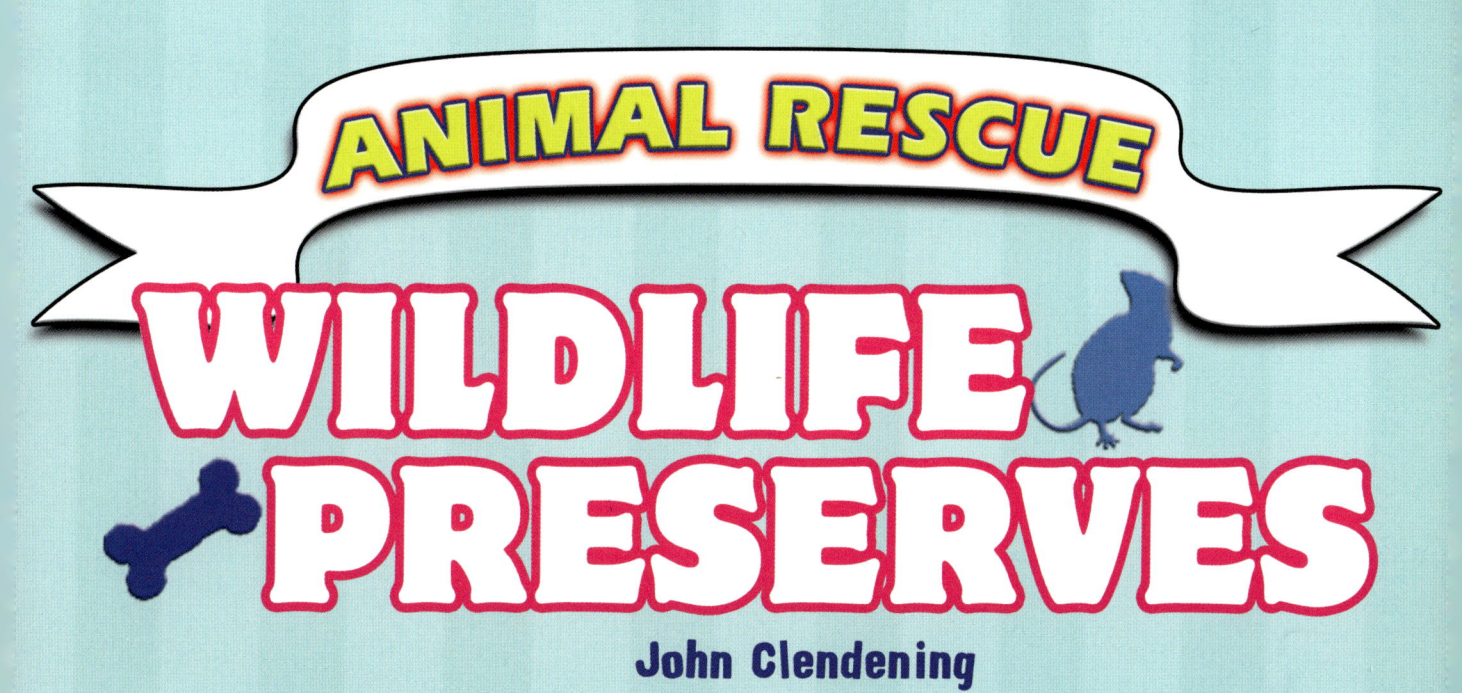

PowerKiDS press
New York

Published in 2015 by The Rosen Publishing Group, Inc.
29 East 21st Street, New York, NY 10010

Copyright © 2015 by The Rosen Publishing Group, Inc.

All rights reserved. No part of this book may be reproduced in any form without permission in writing from the publisher, except by a reviewer.

First Edition

Produced for Rosen by Cyan Candy, LLC
Editor: Joshua Shadowens
Designer: Erica Clendening, Cyan Candy

Photo Credits: Cover, pp. 5, 6, 7, 8, 9, 10, 11, 13, 14, 15, 17, 18, 19, 21, 22, 25, 26, 27, 28, 29 Shutterstock.com; p. 30 spirit of america/Shutterstock.com.

Library of Congress Cataloging-in-Publication Data

Clendening, John, author.
 Wildlife preserves / by John Clendening. — First edition.
    pages cm — (Animal rescue)
 Includes index.
 ISBN 978-1-4777-7015-3 (library binding) — ISBN 978-1-4777-7016-0 (pbk.) — ISBN 978-1-4777-7017-7 (6-pack)
 1. Wildlife refuges—Juvenile literature. 2. Wildlife conservation—Juvenile literature. 3. Animal rescue—Juvenile literature. I. Title.
 QL83.C54 2015
 333.95'416—dc23
                                    2013047631

Manufactured in the United States of America

CPSIA Compliance Information: Batch #WS14PK8: For Further Information contact Rosen Publishing, New York, New York at 1-800-237-9932

TABLE OF CONTENTS

What Is a Wildlife Preserve? 4

Why the World Needs Preserves 8

Not All Wildlife Preserves Are the Same ... 12

A Brief History of Preserves 16

The Biggest Wildlife Preserve in America .. 20

Preserves Around the World 24

The World Needs Animals 28

Glossary 31

Index 32

Websites 32

WHAT IS A WILDLIFE PRESERVE?

Wildlife preserves are protected areas for the **conservation** of wild animals. Preserves allow animals to live in their natural **habitat** without threat from people. Some preserves are man-made to look like the natural habitats of the animals that live in them. This helps if the preserves are far away from the animals' real habitats.

The Earth is home to all of us. All animals, including humans, need a place to live, water to drink, and food to eat. All animals are part of a complex and connected web of life.

Animal Rescue!

Ecosystems are made up of all the animals and plants in a particular place. These living things depend on one another for things they need, such as food or nutrients and even gases. What affects one part of an ecosystem affects all the other parts.

Chital, also known as spotted deer, are native to the woods of India. However, people have introduced them into other countries including America, Croatia, and Chile.

5

Throughout history and all over the world, humans have changed their **environment**. People must clear away plants and animals from land to farm it or to build buildings on it. When humans destroy animals' natural homes, it is called habitat loss.

There are hundreds of wildlife preserves in the world. Some were created to replace lost habitats. Most have been created to make sure that certain habitats will never be lost entirely.

Adult male elephants are the largest land creatures on earth weighing up to 12,000 pounds (5,443 kg). They have 40,000 muscles just in their trunks alone, and can be 10 feet tall (3 m).

Human beings have developed much of the planet for our own needs, but there are still many large areas we have left in their natural states so animals can thrive.

The world's largest wildlife preserves are created and managed by the governments of countries. Many smaller preserves are created by people or organizations that are passionate about wildlife conservation. Some small preserves have been created to provide homes for rescued wild animals.

WHY THE WORLD NEEDS PRESERVES

Wildlife preserves ensure that some areas remain unaffected by people. People alter and sometimes even harm the environment and animals' natural habitats. This can cause **species** to become **endangered**, or at risk of dying out. Even worse, it can cause them to become **extinct**. Extinct species are those that have disappeared forever.

To solve some problems that humans have caused animals, we now consider the needs of animals much

This African buffalo lives in the Kruger National Park in South Africa. These buffaloes are big, strong, unpredictable, and even capable of defending themselves against lion attacks!

Protected wetlands like this one in the state of Missouri are home to many different types of animals. Birds like ducks and geese depend on wetlands for their survival.

more as we construct buildings and roads and plan our cities. For example, we now may designate land in a neighborhood or community to protect in its natural state. We might set aside a piece of wetland, or watery area, to leave undeveloped so that the animals that live there won't lose their homes. This is a kind of preserve.

People are always learning more about the needs of the many different animals with which we share the planet.

A compound found inside dogfish sharks can fight some viruses that cause human diseases. Scientists are now studying this compound looking for new cures. We never know where in nature important cures can come from. This is another important reason that the world needs to protect animals and their habitats.

Thousands of rainbow lorikeets visit the Currumbin Wildlife Sanctuary in Australia every day. They are so used to human visitors feeding them that they will eat right out of people's hands.

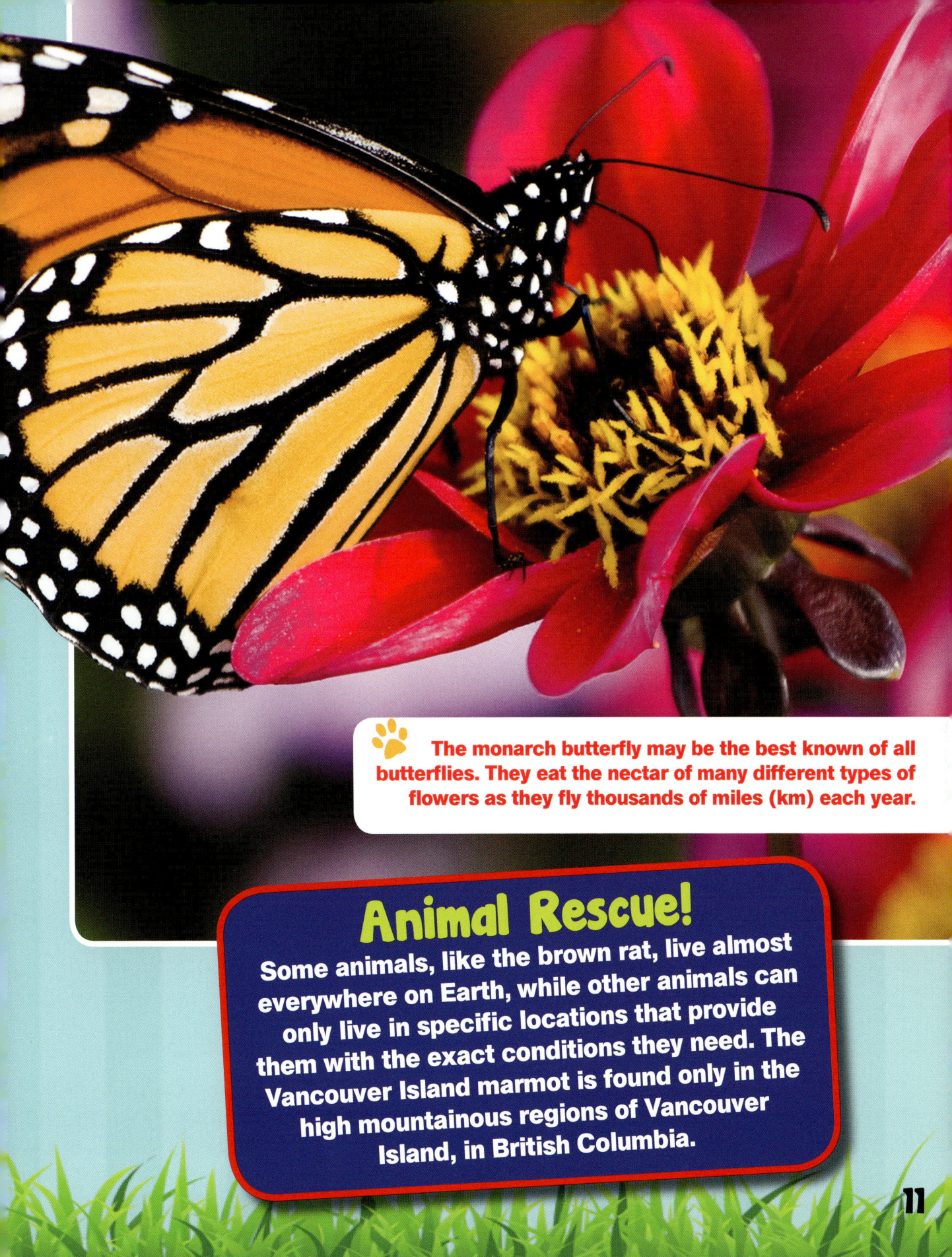

The monarch butterfly may be the best known of all butterflies. They eat the nectar of many different types of flowers as they fly thousands of miles (km) each year.

Animal Rescue!

Some animals, like the brown rat, live almost everywhere on Earth, while other animals can only live in specific locations that provide them with the exact conditions they need. The Vancouver Island marmot is found only in the high mountainous regions of Vancouver Island, in British Columbia.

NOT ALL WILDLIFE PRESERVES ARE THE SAME

The largest wildlife preserves on Earth are created and managed on public lands by national governments. Some of these preserves are so big that they contain entire **ecosystems**. A large wildlife preserve can be home to hundreds, or even thousands, of different animal species.

Some forests, mountain ranges, and deserts are so big they reach into parts of two or more countries. Countries create borders between themselves to define their political boundaries. However, animals don't know about or care about these borders. They simply go where they must within their habitat to meet their own needs.

Some governments work together to create and manage huge wildlife preserves. These preserves might extend into multiple countries. One such preserve is Glacier National Park, which covers land in two countries, including the US and Canada.

The Denali National Park in Alaska is larger than the state of Massachusetts. Inside this park is Mount McKinley, the highest mountain in North America. It is 20,237 feet (6,168 m) tall!

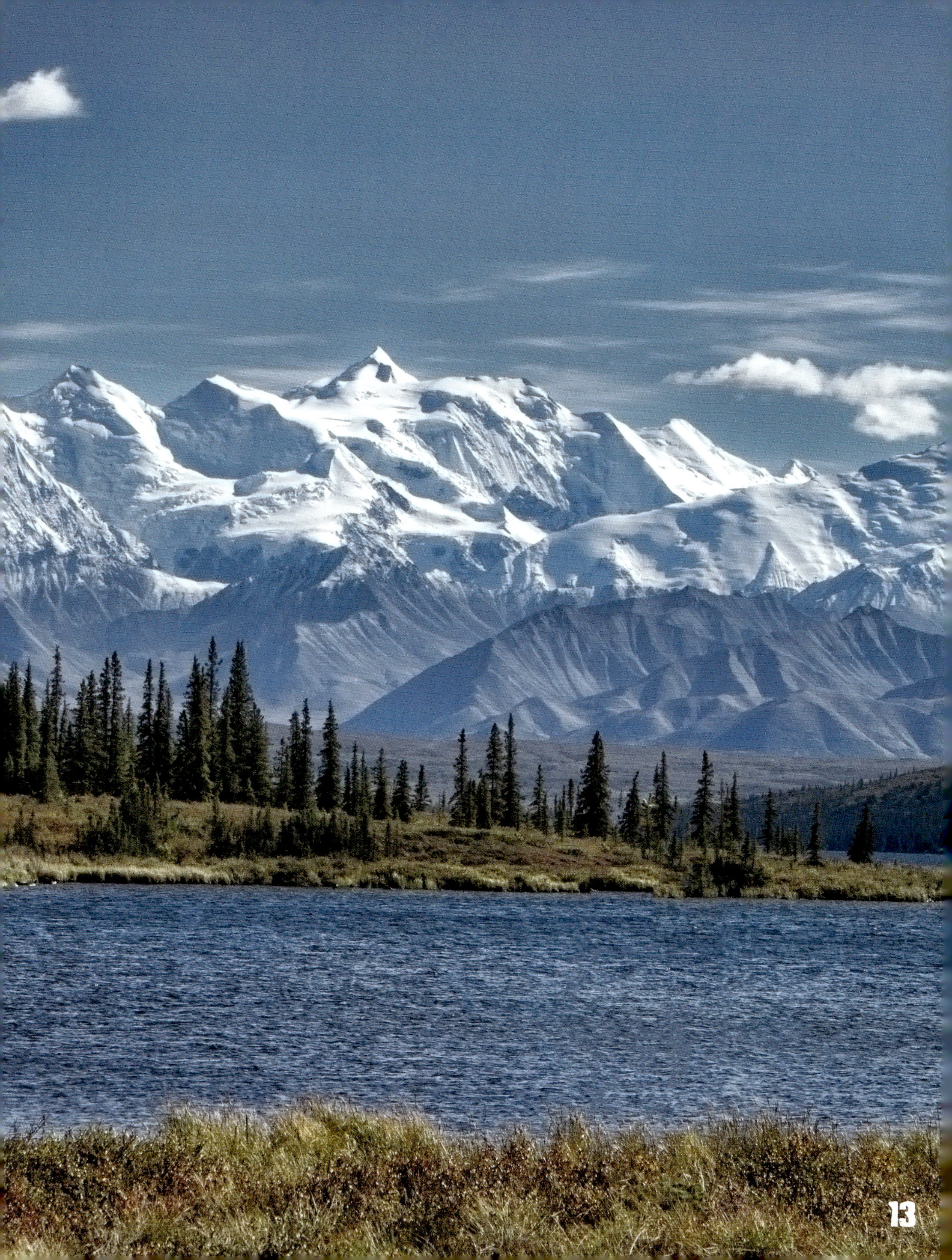

Conservation groups and private citizens create preserves on private land. Some small preserves exist to provide **sanctuary** for animals that have been rescued from people who try raising wild animals as pets.

People have kept cats and dogs as pets for thousands of years. Over time, these animals have evolved to rely on and to live with humans, and have become domesticated, which is the opposite of wild.

Sloths are one of the slowest animals. They spend most of their lives hanging upside down in trees. On the ground, their average speed is about 6.5 feet (2 m) per minute.

Cheetahs are the fastest land animals. They can run as fast as 75 miles per hour (121 km/h) and go from 0 to 62 miles per hour (0–100 km/h) in 3 seconds. That's fast!

Animal Rescue!

Over the last few decades many big cat sanctuaries have been created in America to take care of lions and tigers that people have tried to keep as pets. Lion and tiger cubs are very small and cute, but they grow up to be very large and can be dangerous.

When people try to make pets out of wild animals, it might be fine while the animal is a baby and very small. However, when the animal grows up, it becomes larger and stronger. A wild animal kept as a pet might attack its owner or escape and attack others.

A BRIEF HISTORY OF PRESERVES

Modern people did not create the first preserves. About 2,300 years ago, King Devanampiya Tissa created history's first known wildlife sanctuary in Sri Lanka. He commanded his subjects not to harm any animals or trees within a large jungle area he controlled. This preserve still exists today. Since then, preserves have been created all over the world. They protect the habitats of millions of animals and ensure their continued **survival**.

Before most people lived in cities, communities were much smaller. There were fewer people competing for resources with animals in any particular area.

Today, the human population grows larger every year, mostly in cities. This causes cities to expand in size, taking land from wildlife. We now have—and need—more wildlife preserves than ever before in history.

Tam Coc Natural Preserve in Vietnam

In the United States, wildlife preserves were first established in the nineteenth century. At that time people were beginning to notice that we were harming the environment and animals as our young country grew. As America rapidly industrialized, it needed to use more **natural resources**. However, there were few government controls in place to ensure it did not overuse these resources.

Animal Rescue!

The American bison, also known as the American buffalo, was almost hunted to extinction. Before pioneers settled America there were about 60 million bison. By 1890, there were about 750. Due to ongoing conservation efforts and the creation of preserves for them, there were about 360,000 by 2000.

Wood and paper come from trees. Each American uses an amount of wood and paper each year that is equal to a 100 foot (30.5 m) tall tree that is 18 inches (46 cm) around.

Certain animals, such as passenger pigeons and bison, started to disappear as a result of habitat loss and overhunting. To stop this, the United States started to create wildlife preserves all over the country.

THE BIGGEST WILDLIFE PRESERVE IN AMERICA

The Arctic National Wildlife **Refuge** in northeast Alaska is the largest wildlife preserve in the United States. It covers more than 19 million acres (8 million ha)—the size of the whole state of South Carolina! Combined with Canada's Ivvavik and Vuntut national parks, which it borders, it is home to one of the largest protected ecosystems in the entire world.

It is home to a herd of 120,000 caribou and to millions of birds. It is also home to many animals, such as polar bears, grizzly bears, and wolves, that need lots of space. Many other animals live in this wildlife preserve, and they all share its plentiful natural resources.

Animal Rescue!

One acre (.4 ha) is a little smaller than an American football field. There are 90 million acres (36 million ha) in America protected as wildlife preserves under the National Refuge System, with about 77 million of the acres (31 million ha) in Alaska. Alaska is the biggest state with the most undeveloped land of all the states.

🐾 **There are currently no roads within or leading into the Arctic National Wildlife Refuge. Visitors must either walk into the park or arrive by airplane to enjoy its natural beauty.**

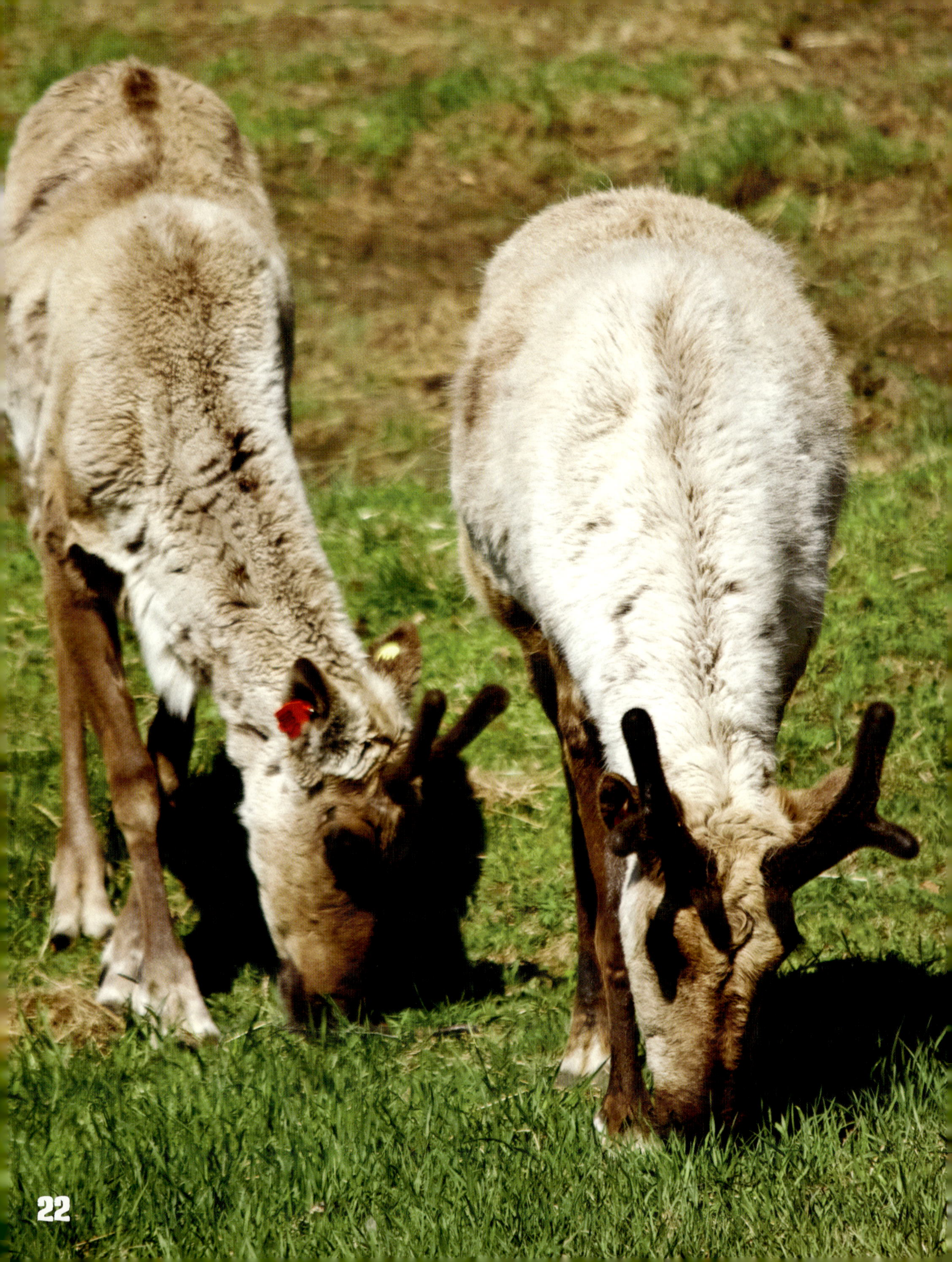

This area of the world contains large deposits of natural resources, such as oil and natural gas. Oil and natural gas are used to make electricity and plastics. Oil is also used to make gasoline for our cars, ships, and planes.

For many years, people have debated whether or not **development** should take place here to extract these valuable natural resources. Until we develop better technologies to provide us with the power we need, we still must rely on oil and gas. However, if we extract these resources from the Earth in these protected areas, we might damage or destroy habitats. And that could lead to endangerment or extinction for the species that live there.

Caribous only eat plants. When the plants they eat are buried under snow, they can scoop away the snow with their hooves which are hollowed out for just this purpose.

PRESERVES AROUND THE WORLD

Countries all over the world set aside land and bodies of water for wildlife preserves. Costa Rica is one of the countries with the most **biodiversity** on Earth. The Monteverde Cloud Forest Reserve there contains over 26,000 acres of lush jungle and crystal clear rivers and waterfalls. It is home to more than 100 different mammals, 400 species of birds, and over 2,500 types of plants. Preserves like this one are not only places off limits to development, they are also important places to learn about how our planet works. **Bioprospecting**, the search for new cures for diseases, is a major activity here.

Animal Rescue!

Sloths' bodies make excellent habitats for many organisms. A sloth may be home to cockroaches, moths, and beetles, among other insects. The green color of a sloth's fur is caused by fungi and algae growing in it.

Sloth in Costa Rica

Australia also has much biodiversity. Many animals live in an area called the Great Barrier Reef, off the coast in the Coral Sea. This collection of more than 2,900 individual reefs is the world's largest structure of living organisms, made up of billions of individual corals, which are small marine animals.

Many endangered species live here. Over 1,500 different fish species and more than 5,000 species of mollusks (shellfish) can be found living in and around the reefs. The reef is also home to numerous exotic marine

Coral reefs all around the world are very popular places for scuba divers to visit underwater because so many different species of colorful fish live in and around them.

🐾 **Jellyfish live in every ocean on Earth and come in many different sizes and shapes. They have been around for 500-700 million years and most are made up of 95-98% water.**

creatures and many species of sharks, whales, dolphins, and other large marine animals.

Together with over 900 islands, this giant reef system covers over 133,000 square miles (344,500 sq km). A large part of this area called the Great Barrier Reef Marine Park is a protected marine animal reserve.

THE WORLD NEEDS ANIMALS

Humans are just one of the millions of animal species on Earth, but the impact of our development on the planet is enormous. Scientists do not know how many other different species exist because we still have not discovered them all.

Hundreds of new species are discovered every year. Current estimates suggest 80% of the land animals and 90% of the marine animals on Earth still await discovery.

Humans are made up of over 50% water. Water is essential to all life so it is extremely important that we always protect all of the water on our planet.

Bottlenose dolphins have been known to help people in dangerous situations. One case was reported where a group of dolphins protected a swimmer who was being hunted by a shark.

Oceans provide 95% of the livable habitat on the planet, yet 95% of the oceans remain unexplored.

Think about how many different kinds of mammals, birds, reptiles, fishes, insects, and other living things we have already identified. Then consider that for each one we do know about, there could be eight or nine that we do not know about yet.

As we continue to learn about and explore the Earth, it is important for us to remember that we share the planet with millions of other animals. We all need habitat, and resources for our survival. Humans are unique because our activities can **threaten** the world more than the activities of any other species. We have an important responsibility to all the other species on Earth.

Wildlife preserves protect the habitats of other animals from our development. Creating and managing them is an important way we can ensure that all animals continue to survive into the future alongside us.

Humans are animals, too, and we all have to share the Earth's natural resources. Wildlife preserves help to make sure that we all continue to exist together into the future.

GLOSSARY

biodiversity (by-oh-dih-VER-sih-tee) The number of different types of living things that are found in a certain place on Earth.

bioprospecting (by-oh-PRAH-spek-ting) Searching for substances that are produced by living organisms and may be of medical or commercial value.

conservation (kon-sur-VAY-shun) Protecting something from harm.

development (dih-VEH-lup-mint) Growth.

ecosystems (EE-koh-sis-temz) Communities of living things and the surroundings in which they live.

endangered (in-DAYN-jerd) Describing an animal whose species or group has almost all died out.

environment (en-VY-ern-ment) Everything that surrounds human beings and other organisms and everything that makes it possible for them to live.

extinct (ik-STINGKT) No longer existing.

habitat (HA-buh-tat) The surroundings where an animal or a plant naturally lives.

natural resources (NA-chuh-rul REE-sors-ez) Things in nature that can be used by people.

refuge (REH-fyooj) A place that gives shelter or security.

sanctuary (SANK-choo-weh-ree) A place where people or animals are kept safe.

species (SPEE-sheez) A single kind of living thing. All people are one species.

survival (sur-VY-val) Staying alive.

threaten (THREH-tun) To act as though something will possibly cause hurt.

INDEX

B
biodiversity, 24, 26
bioprospecting, 24

C
conservation, 4, 7, 14, 18
compound, 10

D
development, 23, 24, 28, 30
domesticated, 14

E
ecosystem, 4, 12, 20
endangered, 8, 26
environment, 6, 18
extinct, 8, 18, 23

H
habitat, 4, 6, 8, 10, 12, 16, 19, 23, 24, 29, 30

I
industrialized, 18

N
natural resources, 18, 20, 22, 30

P
preserve, 4, 6, 7, 8, 9, 12, 14, 16, 17, 18, 19, 20, 24, 30

R
refuge, 20, 21

S
sanctuary, 10, 14, 16
species, 8, 12, 23, 24, 26, 27, 28, 30
survival, 9, 16, 30

T
threaten, 30

W
wetlands, 9

WEBSITES

Due to the changing nature of Internet links, PowerKids Press has developed an online list of websites related to the subject of this book. This site is updated regularly. Please use this link to access the list: **www.powerkids.com/ares/pres/**